WITHDRAWN

DATE DUE

MAR 3 1993			
DEC 2 1993			
JAN 13 1994			
MAR 15 1994			
GRAD 1994			
JAN 4 1995			
APR 30 1995			
DEC 12 1996			
JUN 01 1998			
JUN 1 1998			
JAN 03 2000			
APR 08 2000			

HIGHSMITH # 45220

TECHNOLOGY IN ACTION

UNDERSEA TECHNOLOGY

Ralph Rayner

The Bookwright Press
New York · 1990

Titles in this series

Aircraft Technology

Car Technology

Farming Technology

Ship Technology

Spacecraft Technology

TV and Video Technology

Train Technology

Undersea Technology

First published in the
United States in 1990 by
The Bookwright Press
387 Park Avenue South
New York, NY 10016

First published in 1990
Wayland (Publishers) Ltd
61 Western Road, Hove
East Sussex BN3 1JD, England

©Copyright 1990 Wayland (Publishers) Ltd

Library of Congress Cataloging-in-Publication Data
Lambert, Mark.
   Undersea technology / by Mark Lambert.
     p. cm. — (Technology in action)
   Includes bibliographical references.
   Summary: Surveys the technology used in underwater exploration, mining, and oil production, describes submarines, bathyscaphes, and other vehicles, and discusses the protection of the undersea environment.
   ISBN 0-531-18347-5
   1. Ocean engineering — Juvenile literature. [1. Ocean engineering.] I. Title. II. Series
TC1645.L36 1990   90–168
620'.4162—dc20   CIP
                                                 AC

Typeset by Direct Image Photosetting Limited,
Sussex, England
Printed in Italy by G. Canale & C.S.p.A., Turin

Front cover A British Oceanics submersible about to be lifted from the water.

Contents

1	Undersea resources	4
2	Exploring the oceans	6
3	Exploring beneath the seabed	8
4	Shallow-water diving	10
5	Deep-water diving	12
6	Working underwater	16
7	Buoyancy and propulsion	18
8	Remotely operated vehicles	20
9	The submersible	22
10	The submarine	24
11	The bathyscaphe	26
12	Undersea navigation	28
13	Fishing technology	30
14	Offshore oil exploration	32
15	Offshore oil production	34
16	Mining the seafloor	36
17	Energy from the sea	38
18	Protecting the environment	40
19	A future undersea?	42
	Glossary	44
	Further reading	45
	Index	46

1 Undersea resources

Seas and oceans cover more than 70 percent of the Earth's surface. Their waters, and the seafloor beneath, contain many valuable and important resources. Before we look at undersea technology, we need to understand a little more about the oceans and the resources that lie hidden deep beneath their waters.

It is only during the last hundred years or so that detailed undersea exploration has been possible. Before this time almost nothing was known about the really deep waters where sunlight does not penetrate. It was not until 1872, and the four-year expedition of the British ship HMS *Challenger*, that the systematic study of the oceans began and the science of oceanography was born.

Since the voyage of the *Challenger*, the technological advances of the twentieth century have made possible the penetration and exploration of even the deepest parts of the oceans. Technology has also made possible detailed mapping of the oceans and exploration of their different resources.

It is now known that there are three basic levels in the oceans. Around the coasts of continents, there are the gently sloping shallow seas of the continental shelf, with water depths of up to a few hundred yards. These shelves are a part of the continental land mass. They may extend only a short distance from land (for example, the continental shelf off Chile is only a few miles wide) or they may cover very extensive areas (the continental shelf off Siberia extends over 620 miles (1,000 km) offshore in places).

At the limit of the continental shelf is the continental slope. This is the true edge of the

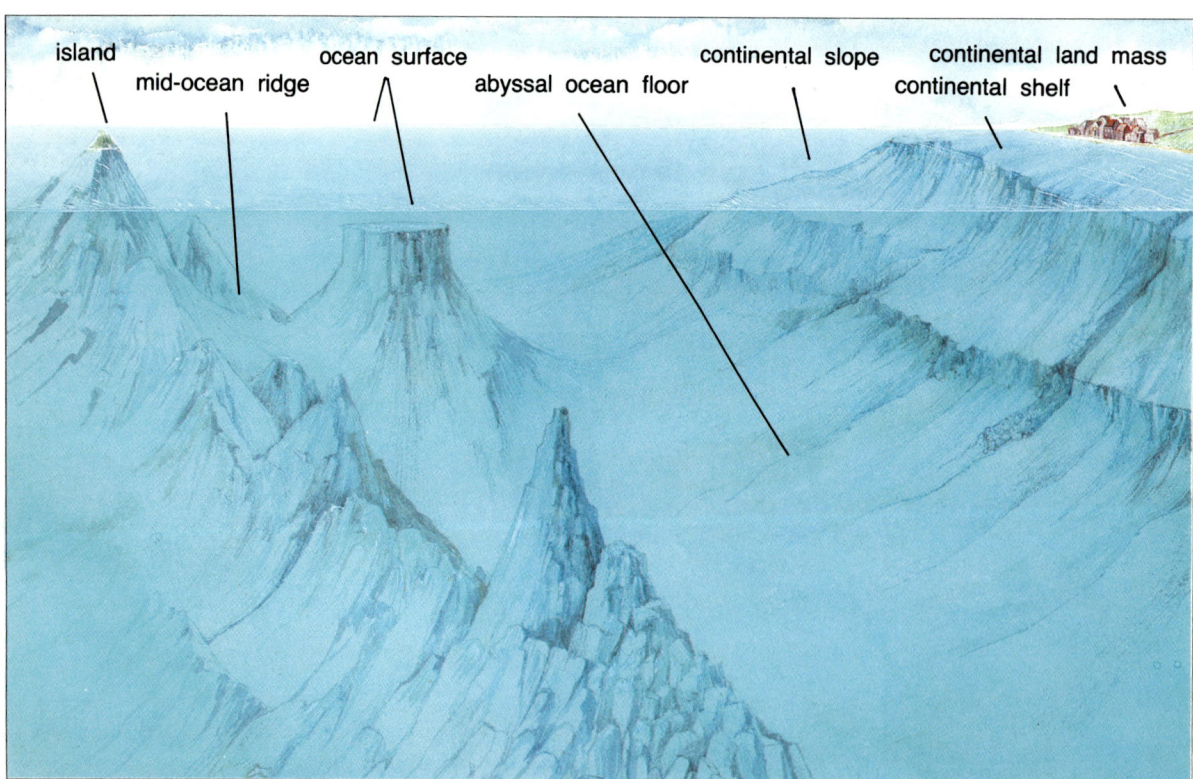

A gas drilling rig off the coast of Norway. Oil and gas are just two of the valuable undersea resources that can be extracted thanks to modern technology.

continent. The slope leads down to the abyssal ocean, whose average depth is about 2½ miles (4 km). Much of the abyssal ocean floor is flat and featureless, but in some areas the flat plain is broken by hills and isolated mountain peaks. Prominent features of the deep ocean floor are the mid-ocean ridges, which are huge mountain ranges with peaks reaching up to 6 miles (10 km) high. In some locations, these peaks reach the surface of the ocean and form islands, such as Iceland.

The oceans and seas are highly important for the resources they contain. Besides the more than 70 million tons of fish caught each year, they provide us with valuable oil and gas from beneath the seabed and energy produced from tides. It is also known that deposits of valuable minerals such as manganese are to be found on the seabed.

Exploiting these resources brings with it special problems, however. There is the obvious difficulty of humans breathing underwater, as well as the problems of high pressure and the corrosive properties of seawater. That we have come as far as we have, and will surely go further, in exploiting these resources is largely due to the development of highly sophisticated undersea technologies.

2 Exploring the oceans

At the time of the voyage of HMS *Challenger*, toward the end of the nineteenth century, few undersea instruments existed. It is only with the technological advances that have taken place in the twentieth century that it has become possible to build sophisticated instruments for studying the oceans.

There are special problems to be overcome when building instruments to use under the sea. Seawater is corrosive, so great care must be taken to protect underwater instruments. This requires the use of special corrosion-resistant materials such as stainless steel and special metal alloys. The great pressure exerted by deep water is another problem. Instruments must be housed in pressure-resistant casings if they are to survive at depth.

The revolution in micro-electronics has allowed many sensitive undersea instruments to be designed and put into use beneath the seas. Oceanographers use these instruments to measure tides, waves, currents and the temperature and salinity (saltiness) of seawater.

Before the development of electronics, the depth of ocean waters was measured by lowering a weight, known as a sounding lead, until it reached the seabed. This method is very slow and laborious, especially in deep water, but the development of echo sounders in the 1920s made measuring the depth of the oceans a good deal easier. Echo sounders transmit sound waves through the water and detect the echoes of the waves when they are reflected back from the seabed. Because it is possible to measure the speed of sound in seawater, the depth of the water can easily be figured out from the time taken for a sound wave to reach the bottom and for its echo to be reflected back to the surface. Echo sounders can take continuous measurements of depth from a moving vessel, so their use has made it possible to chart large areas of the seabed quite quickly.

Cameras that are to be used at depth need to be housed in pressure-resistant casings. Powerful flashguns are also needed to light up the dark waters for photography.

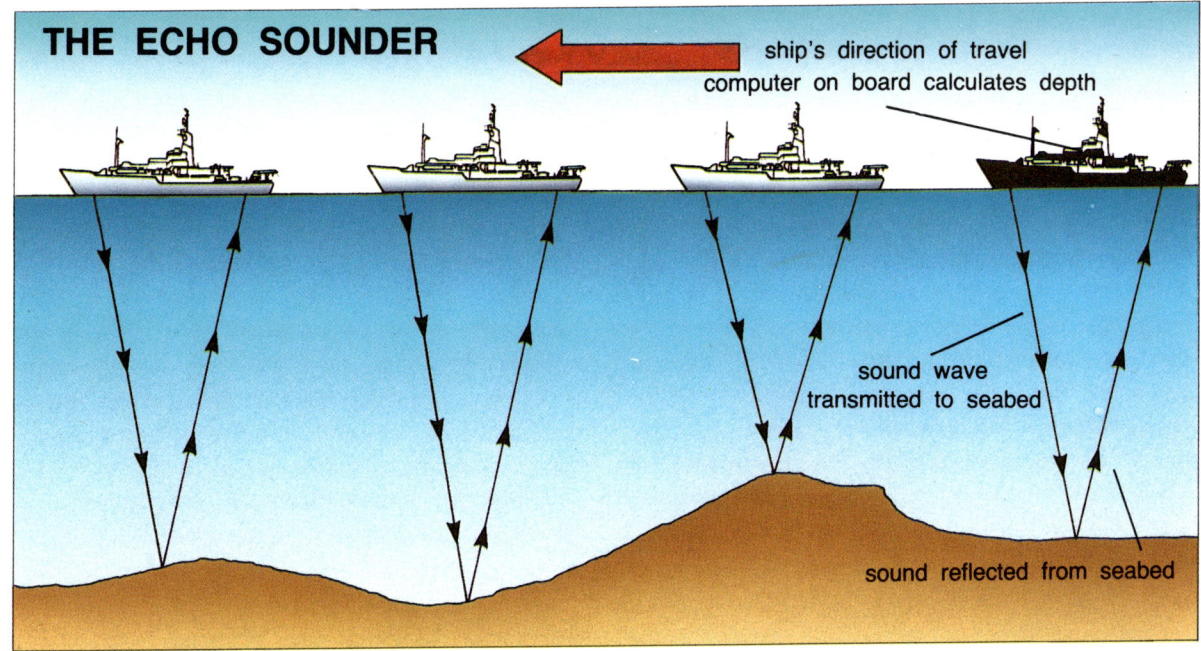

THE ECHO SOUNDER

ship's direction of travel
computer on board calculates depth
sound wave transmitted to seabed
sound reflected from seabed

Charting the depth of the oceans is, however, only part of the story. We also need to know what sort of material covers the seabed. Is the seabed solid rock or is it covered with mud, sand or gravel? One way of answering this question is to collect samples of seabed material. Samples can be collected using mechanical grabs lowered to the seabed. Like the use of the sounding lead for depth measurements, though, this is a slow process.

A solution to this problem is to use underwater cameras to take pictures of the seabed. Both still cameras and video cameras may be used underwater provided that they are housed in special pressure-proof containers. For use at depths where light does not penetrate, such camera systems must be equipped with powerful lights.

There is, though, a serious problem with using cameras underwater. Above water, light travels faster and penetrates farther through the atmosphere than sound does. However, underwater, light can travel only relatively short distances because of the optical properties of water and the effects of small particles that are usually found in seawater. It is because of this that sunlight is capable of penetrating to the seabed only in shallow water.

Because of the poor penetration of light in seawater, underwater cameras can see for only a very limited distance. In contrast to light, sound travels very well in seawater. Using developments of the technology behind the echo sounder, it is possible to produce sound-generated images of large areas of the seabed. This method of producing images of the seafloor is known as sonar imaging, and the instrument used to collect such images is a side-scan sonar.

The principle of the side-scan sonar is quite simple. Fan-shaped beams of sound are sent out from either side of a torpedo-like housing (known as a "towfish") that is towed behind a ship. The echoes reflected from the seafloor are received by the towfish. The nature of the seabed (whether it is, for example, rock, sand or gravel) affects the quality of the echo received by the towfish. The echoes can be processed electronically on board the ship to produce an image of the seafloor.

One of the most advanced and sophisticated side-scan sonars is GLORIA (Geological Long Range Inclined Asdic). It scans the seafloor with two sonar beams that "illuminate" the seabed with sound up to 18 or 19 miles (30 km) to either side of the towfish.

3 Exploring beneath the seabed

Much of our knowledge of the geological structures beneath the seabed has been gained using a technique known as seismic surveying. A loud bang or shock wave generated underwater at the stern of a seismic survey ship travels through the water to the seabed and then through to the rocks below. A long row of very sensitive underwater microphones, called hydrophones, is towed behind the ship to detect the sound waves reflected back from the rock layers beneath the seabed. Signals from the hydrophones are processed electronically on board to provide information about the time taken by the sound to reach different rock layers.

If a series of closely spaced shock waves is generated from a steadily moving survey ship, a continuous record of the time taken for the sound to reach and return from the different layers of rock beneath the seabed can be produced on a special printer. As long as the speed of sound through the different rock layers is known, this record can be turned into a continuous cross-section of the seabed showing the thickness of the different rock layers.

Many different devices are used to generate the shock waves that are such an important part of underwater seismics. In some cases explosives provide the shock waves, but more usually the sound is generated in more controllable ways, such as by making high-voltage sparks underwater or by using compressed air in a special device called an airgun.

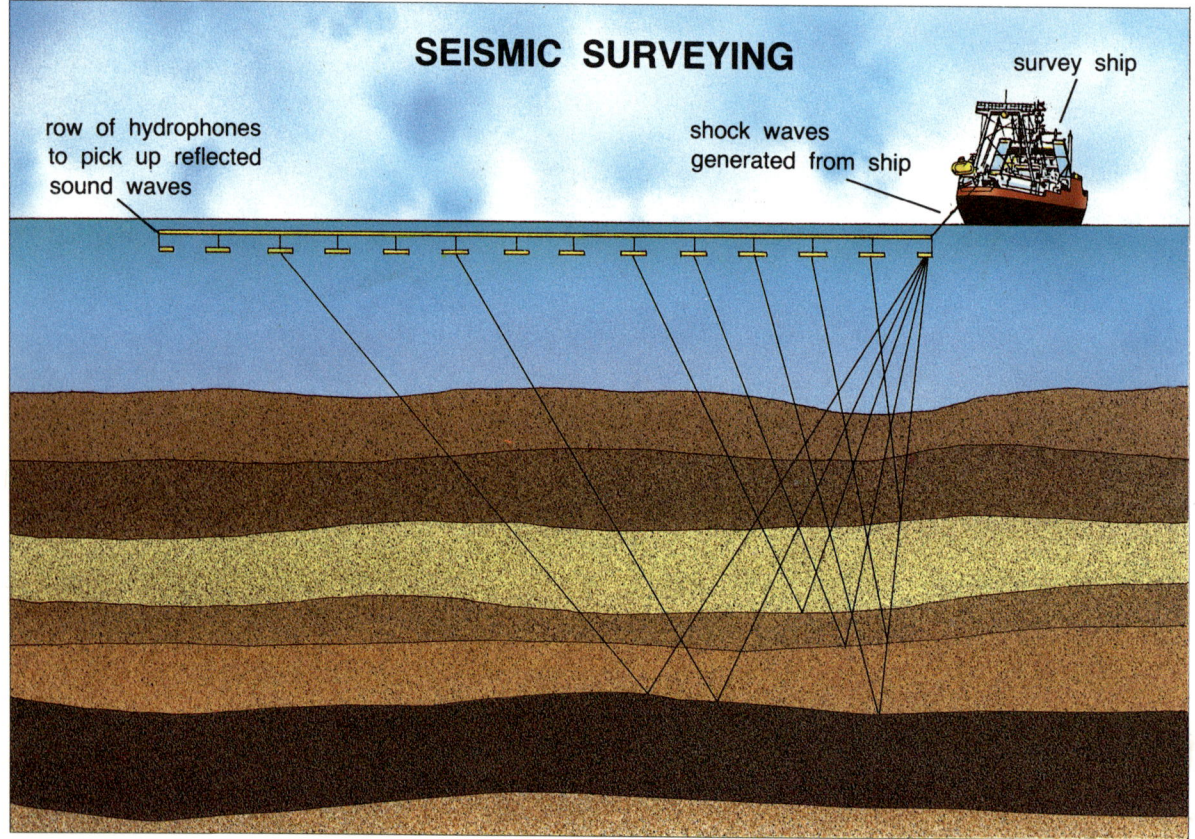

SEISMIC SURVEYING

row of hydrophones to pick up reflected sound waves

shock waves generated from ship

survey ship

A technician views seismic information at a laboratory in the United States.

If very detailed information about the rocks below the seabed is required, this can be obtained only by drilling through the seabed to obtain rock samples. This is a difficult and costly operation, especially in deep water. The tools used to drill into the seabed are very similar to those used to drill on land. A drilling bit is attached to the end of a series of drill pipes until it reaches the seabed. Once it has reached the seabed, the bit is rotated by a drive motor at the surface. As the drill goes down into the seabed, more drill pipes are screwed on behind it. In this way holes can be drilled to depths of over a mile into the seabed.

There are a number of difficult problems to solve when drilling into rocks beneath the deep ocean floor. Because it is not possible to anchor in such deep water, an alternative means, known as dynamic positioning, is needed to hold the vessel in position over the drilling site. This involves the drilling site being marked by seabed sonar beacons called transponders. These beacons respond to pulses of sound sent out by the ship, emitting a return pulse, which is received by hydrophones on the ship's hull. Computers on board the ship use information about the time taken for sound to travel to and from the transponders to determine the ship's position relative to the drilling location. These computers control special propellers called thrusters, which are used to keep the ship in the correct position over the drill site.

4 Shallow-water diving

The earliest device to aid diving in shallow waters was described by the Greek philosopher Aristotle around 300 BC. It consisted of a kind of upturned bucket that trapped air and allowed a diver to breathe for a short time underwater. Improvements on this idea in the 1700s led to the development of a diving bell supplied with air from pumps at the surface. These early diving bells were clumsy to use and made it difficult for the diver to move freely underwater. The invention of the diving helmet or "hard hat" in the 1820s was the first significant step in overcoming these problems.

The first practical Self-Contained Underwater Breathing Apparatus (SCUBA) was developed by Jacques-Yves Cousteau in 1943. This was the first piece of diving equipment that allowed the diver to swim freely underwater without the need for hoses to supply air from the surface. SCUBA equipment relies on a special valve, called a demand valve, which Cousteau invented. It reduces the air pressure from a cylinder of compressed air to a pressure just sufficient to deliver air when the diver inhales.

A diver breathing air can work only in waters less than about 200 feet (61 m) deep. Below this

Above left A late-nineteenth-century diver. Air was supplied to his helmet by a surface pump. **Above right** SCUBA equipment allows this diver to move freely.

This diver is wearing a decompression computer on his wrist. The device tells him how long he should take to return to the surface in order to avoid the bends.

depth, the gases that make up air begin to have poisonous effects because of the pressure at which they are being breathed. At high pressures, the nitrogen gas in air begins to affect the diver's brain, causing a sensation very similar to drunkenness. This condition is known as nitrogen narcosis. Oxygen poisoning also occurs at high pressure with the tissues of the body receiving too much of the gas. At depths greater than about 260 feet (80 m), this poisoning can be fatal.

A further problem facing the diver is "the bends." When air is breathed under pressure, more gases than normal are dissolved in the blood and tissues. The bends occur when the pressure is suddenly reduced as the diver surfaces. If this reduction happens too rapidly, the gases may form bubbles in the blood and tissues, causing severe pain and, in some cases, death. The bends can only be avoided by a very controlled ascent to the surface that is slow enough to prevent bubbles from forming. The longer or deeper the dive has been, the slower must be the diver's ascent. Coming back to the surface from very deep or long dives, the diver must stop for a prescribed time at a number of carefully chosen depths. This procedure is known as decompression.

5 Deep-water diving

Preparing to dive from a Nigerian oil platform. The pipe is an umbilical.

The depth limitations of air diving can be overcome by having the diver breathe a special mixture of gases. With deep-water diving, the oxygen poisoning problem is overcome by reducing the concentration of oxygen in the breathing mixture. Nitrogen narcosis is avoided by replacing the nitrogen in the breathing mixture with another gas, helium. Helium does not have the toxic effects of nitrogen, but it does have one strange side-effect: it raises the pitch of the diver's voice. Deep-water divers usually have voice communications links with the surface and, in order for their speech to be understood, the pitch of their voices must be reduced to a normal level electronically.

As dive depth, and hence pressure, increases,

Left The special mask this diver is wearing recycles the expensive helium gas the diver breathes instead of letting it be exhaled into the water.

Right The diving control room of a diving support vessel in the North Sea. The supervisor gives directions from here to the divers working below.

more and more breathing gas is needed for each breath. A cylinder that lasts for 30 minutes at 33 feet (10 m) would not last three minutes at 650 feet (198 m). For this reason, deep-water divers carry a cylinder only for emergency use. Their main supply of breathing gas comes through a pipe (called an umbilical), which is connected to the surface or to a diving bell. Besides supplying breathing gas, the umbilical usually includes a pipe to carry hot water to the diver's suit to keep him warm and a telephone line for communication with the surface.

After only a few minutes at a depth of, say, 650 feet (198 m), a diver would need hours of decompression before being able to return to the surface. For deep-water diving, it is safer and

Above Divers descend to the work site in a diving bell. **Right** Passing time in a decompression chamber.

more practical to house the diver at the same pressure as his working depth than for the diver to go through many lengthy decompressions. This method of diving is known as "saturation diving," because the diver's body tissues become saturated with breathing gas.

When saturation divers are not working underwater, they live in a sealed chamber at an atmospheric pressure equal to that at their normal working depth. To enter the water, the divers transfer, still under pressure, to a diving bell which is used to lower them to the work site. After a period of work, they return to the surface in the diving bell and are once again transferred to the chamber. In this way, divers can move between the surface and their work location without the need for decompression. On completion of the deep-water task or at the end of their "shift" (which may be several weeks in length), they are decompressed in a pressure

chamber, where the pessure is gradually reduced over a period of several days.

There is another way of avoiding the problems of breathing gas at high pressure. This involves enclosing the diver in a rigid suit that is strong enough to withstand the external water pressure. The diver is then able to breathe air at normal atmospheric pressure. A good example of a one-atmosphere suit is the Jim suit (named after Jim Jarrett, who was responsible for early test dives in this type of suit).

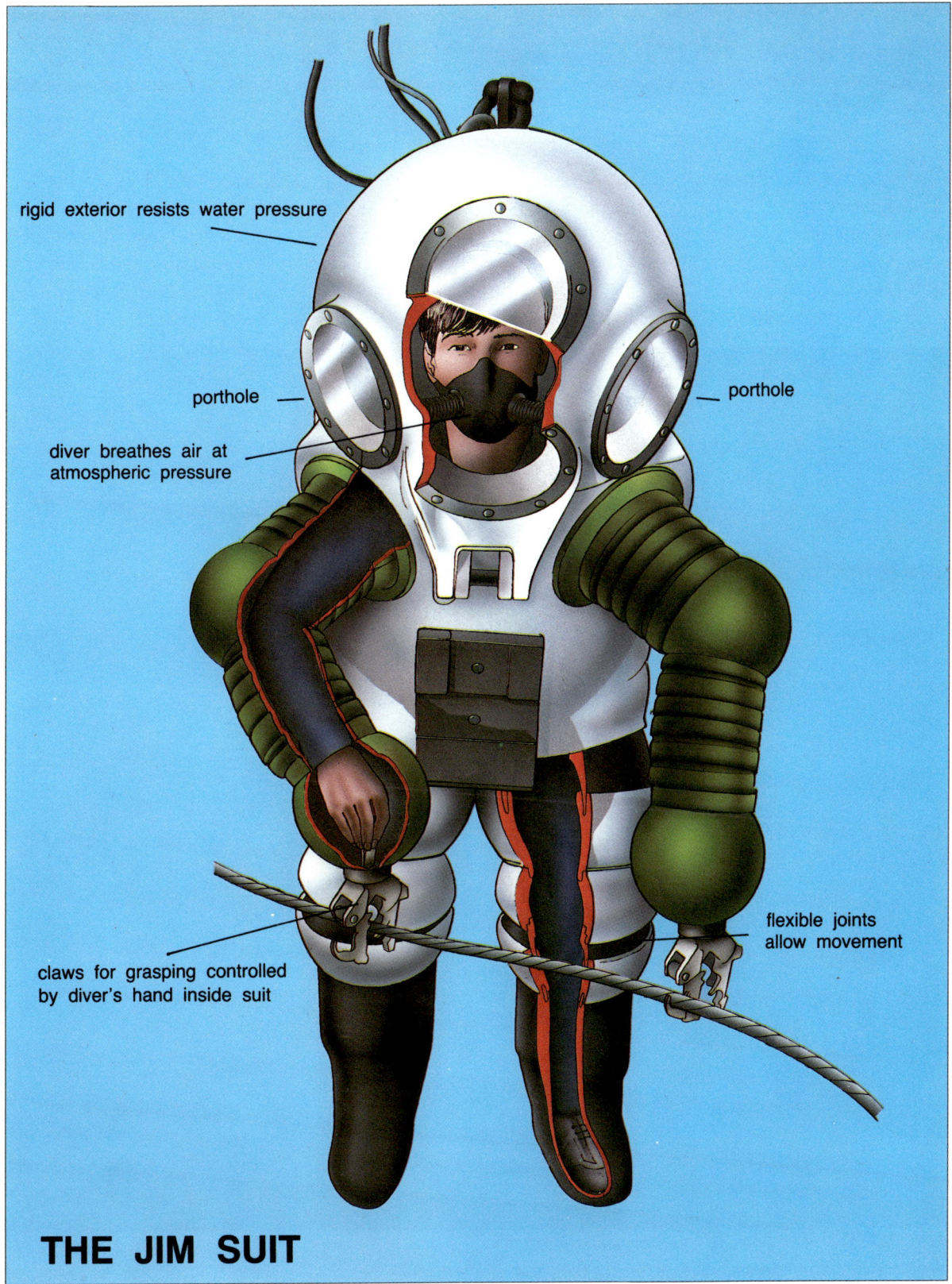

6 Working underwater

Divers are called upon to carry out a wide variety of underwater tasks. Typical jobs that they might perform include the cleaning, inspection and repair of underwater structures such as offshore oil production platforms.

To assist them in these tasks, divers require a number of special tools. These tools must be designed to work effectively underwater without risk to the diver. This means most electrically powered tools are unsuitable, since seawater is a good conductor of electricity and there would be a high risk of the diver's being electrocuted.

A diver using an underwater cutting tool called a thermal lance.

This cleaning tool is powered by hydraulics.

For this reason, it has been necessary to develop power tools that are driven by pneumatic power. Many pneumatic tools are similar to those driven by electricity, except that they use air motors. An air motor consists of a rotor contained in a small chamber. Compressed air enters the chamber and causes the rotor to turn, and this rotation is then used to drive the underwater tool. Tools that a diver might use include power wrenches, drills and grinders.

High-pressure water is also used to power some divers' devices. Pressurized water jets driven by powerful pumps are used to excavate the seafloor and to clear sediment and pieces of debris from around wrecks or structures that are to be repaired.

One job that divers are often required to undertake is the inspection of underwater welds to check that no minute cracks are forming that might make a structure like an oil platform unsafe. The diver first has to clean the weld using underwater cleaning tools to remove marine growths such as barnacles and seaweeds. A test device that detects minute cracks using a beam of very high-pitched sound is then run over the structure. The diver knows if there are any cracks present by the way in which the sound is changed as it passes through the metal.

If any serious cracking is discovered, it may be necessary for divers to repair the weld using underwater welding equipment. This welding equipment is similar to the equipment used on land. Welding torches work underwater because they have their own supply of oxygen that keeps the flame burning even when the torch has been submerged.

7 Buoyancy and propulsion

There are many different types of undersea vessels, each of them designed to perform a variety of underwater tasks. The design of each reflects the type of tasks it undertakes. Perhaps the most familiar vessel is the naval submarine, while others include remotely operated robot vehicles used to perform tasks on undersea structures like oil production platforms, manned submersibles used for undersea exploration, and bathyspheres and bathyscaphes, which dive to the very deepest parts of the oceans.

Except for those that are lowered from a surface ship on a cable, all of these different undersea vessels have in common the need to be able to control their position in the water both horizontally and vertically. Untethered vessels must also be able to control their buoyancy in the water in order to be able to leave and return to the surface.

Buoyancy is controlled by ballast tanks. When these are full of air, the submarine or submersible floats on the surface. In order for the

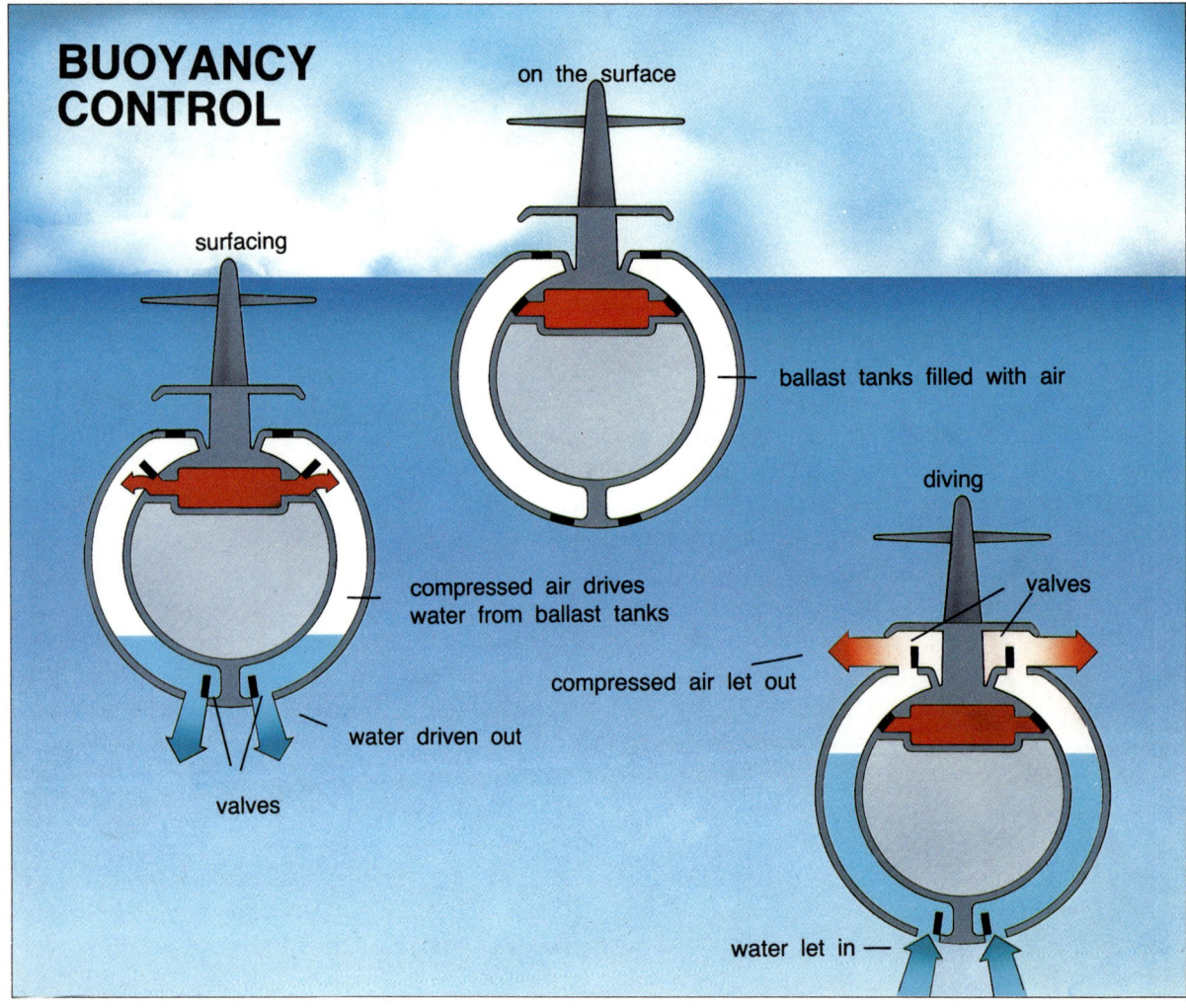

18

vessel to dive, the ballast tanks have to be allowed to fill with seawater, reducing the buoyancy of the vessel and causing it to sink beneath the surface. At the end of the dive, water in the ballast tanks is blown out using compressed air. This increases the buoyancy of the vessel, allowing it to float to the surface.

In most undersea craft, propulsion is generated by means of propellers. The military submarine has only one or two large propellers driven by very powerful motors, which can push the submarine through the water at high speed. Some modern nuclear submarines are capable of traveling at submerged speeds of up to 48 mph (78 kph). Remotely operated vehicles and submersibles, on the other hand, often have a number of small propellers driven by separate electric motors. Fast speeds are not important with vessels of this kind; what is needed is very precise control over their position in the water as they perform their tasks. This control is achieved through having several separate propellers.

Once under the water, the vessel must be capable of being steered, and its depth must be controlled. Submarines and most submersibles are steered by means of a rudder. Up and down motion is controlled by small "wings" called hydroplanes, which are angled to cause the craft to move upward or downward as it is driven through the water.

Submersibles' propellers are generally small to aid maneuverability.

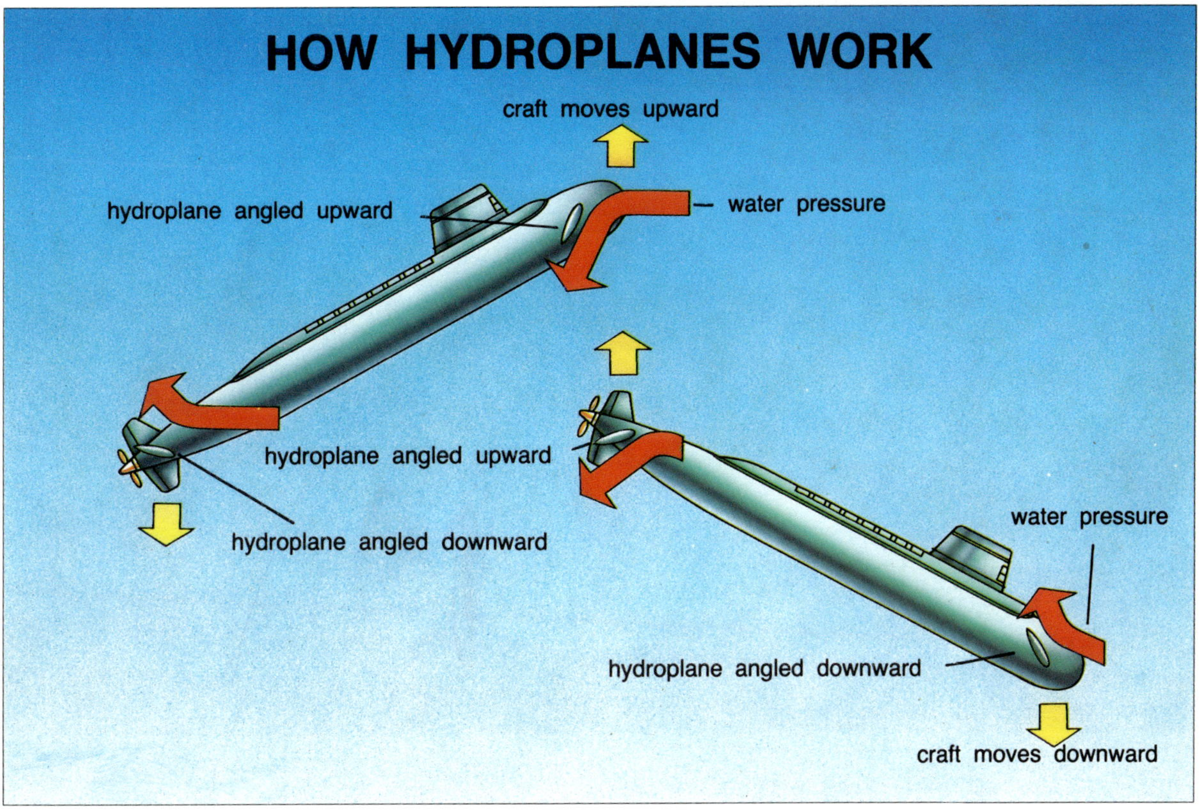

HOW HYDROPLANES WORK

19

8 Remotely operated vehicles

Many underwater tasks are now carried out by robot undersea vehicles operated from the surface. They have the advantage of being able to operate in situations that might be dangerous for a diver. For many tasks, they also offer a less expensive alternative to diving.

Remotely operated vehicles, or ROVs for short, are tethered to the surface by an umbilical cable that carries power and control signals to the vehicle. The umbilical also relays television pictures to the ROV's "pilot" on the surface. The pilot controls the ROV using a joystick control

This ROV is fitted with television cameras for survey work.

that is rather like those that are used with many computer games.

The earliest ROVs were supported on tow cables and had little maneuverability of their own. They were used mostly for carrying underwater camera systems. More recently, though, ROVs have been developed that can be maneuvered using small propellers called thrusters. These are positioned on the vehicle in such a way that they can be used to control both its horizontal and vertical motion. The ROV's mobility and maneuverability in deeper water can be improved by not tethering it directly to the surface but by operating it from an undersea "garage" which is, in turn, suspended from the surface control ship.

ROVs range in size from not much larger than a soccer ball, in which form they are used for observation only, to about the size of a car. This latter type of ROV can carry a variety of tools on robot arms, which the pilot can control from the surface. Tools for grasping, cutting and turning allow ROVs to carry out quite complex underwater tasks.

THE ROV

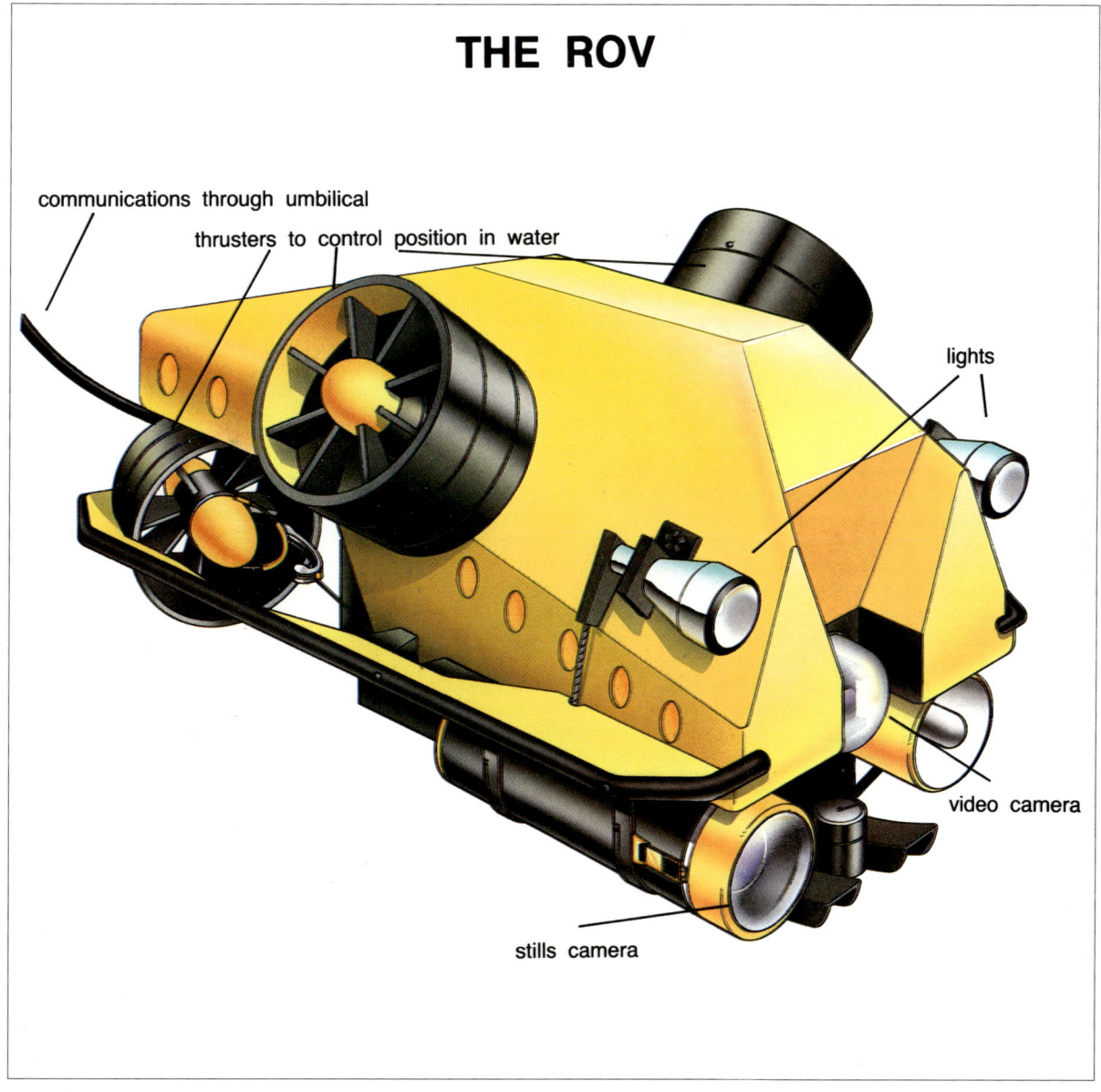

communications through umbilical
thrusters to control position in water
lights
video camera
stills camera

9 The submersible

A submersible is lowered into the sea from its mother ship.

Submersibles are like small submarines and are used for a variety of industrial and scientific applications underwater. Some submersibles are designed to work only in shallow waters, while others can work at depths well beyond the limits for deep-water diving. They carry only a small crew of perhaps one or two people. The crew members sit in a pressure chamber and breathe air at normal atmospheric pressure. Some submersibles also have a second compartment that can be used to transport divers from the surface to their work site. This compartment can be pressurized, allowing the divers to leave the submersible through watertight doors. The pressurized chamber also allows the submersible to return the divers to the surface under pressure once their work is completed. They can then undergo decompression in a surface decompression chamber.

Submersibles are used only for short dives that last no more than a day. They are taken to their work site by a "mother" ship and are launched and recovered from a special gantry at the stern of the ship. Unlike most submarines, whose powerful motors can carry them thousands of miles through the oceans without the need to resurface, submersibles are powered by large battery packs, which must be recharged between dives. This makes them lighter and less costly to build. The battery packs are often attached to the outside of the vessel so that they can be released in an emergency, such as a power failure, which might prevent the craft from surfacing normally. Releasing the battery packs, which can be quite heavy, allows the submersible to float to the surface.

Some submersibles are equipped only with camera systems for underwater observations, while others have mechanical arms called manipulators, which have tools attached to them. Manipulator arms, which are driven by hydraulics, can carry a variety of tools including grabs for taking samples, special controllable claws for grasping, and drilling and cutting tools for carrying out repairs on underwater structures.

Thanks to their maneuverability and the variety of tasks they can perform, submersibles are frequently used for scientific research and exploration. Perhaps the best-known research submersible is one called *Alvin*, which is capable of taking a crew of three to a depth of more than 13,000 feet (4,000 m). *Alvin* was involved in the successful search for the wreck of the *Titanic*. The wreck, at a depth of over 13,000 feet (4,000 m), was photographed by a combination of the submersible *Alvin* and an ROV called *Jason Junior*. *Jason Junior* was attached to *Alvin* by an umbilical cable, which allowed the crew of the submersible to guide the ROV through the wreck, taking photographs as it went.

Alvin, which was involved in the search for the *Titanic*.

10 The submarine

The earliest working submarines were powered by hand-driven propellers and were capable of staying underwater for only a very limited period. One of the first really practical submarines was the French *Narval*, launched in 1899. This small submarine was one of the first to use two sets of propulsion machinery. On the surface, diesel engines propelled the craft and also charged a bank of batteries. Under the water, these batteries were used to power electric motors to drive the propellers. This combination of diesel and electric power was to be the basis of all submarine propulsion up until the 1950s.

Diesel-electric submarines suffer from the disadvantage that they must return to the surface relatively frequently to run their diesel engines and recharge the propulsion batteries. To avoid having the submarine resurface completely, a pair of snorkel tubes are extended in the same way as the periscope. These allow the diesel engines to take in air and to expel their exhaust gases. Snorkel tubes are also used to replenish the breathing air on board the submarine. When the craft is submerged, the breathing air is recycled many times by passing it through devices called "scrubbers."

The world's first nuclear submarine, the American-built *Nautilus*, was launched in 1954.

THE MILITARY NUCLEAR SUBMARINE

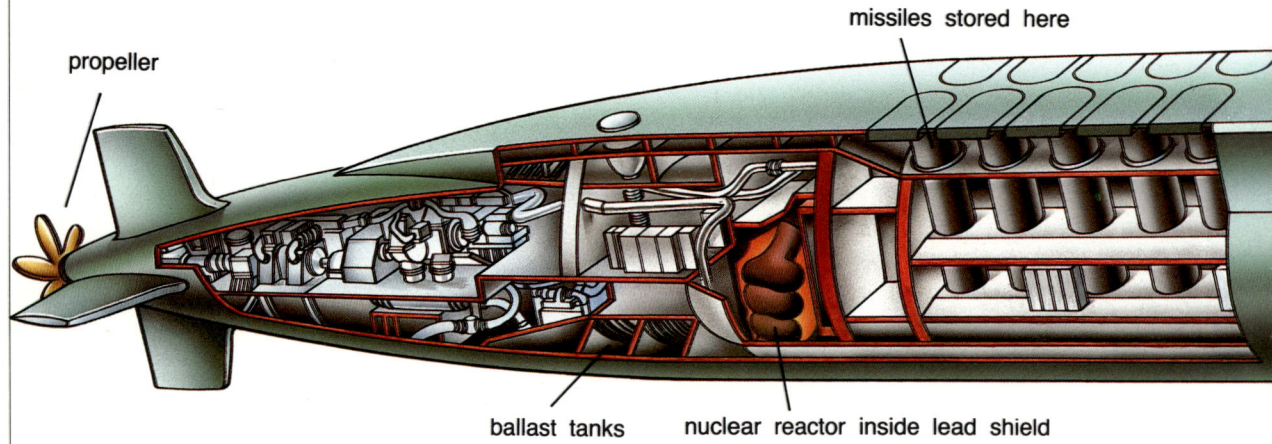

propeller — ballast tanks — nuclear reactor inside lead shield — missiles stored here

A nuclear submarine is propelled by using the heat generated by a nuclear reactor to make steam, which drives a turbine to rotate the propeller. The use of nuclear power has made it possible for submarines to spend very long periods underwater, since nuclear reactors do not produce poisonous exhaust fumes or consume oxygen gas. In a nuclear submarine there is, therefore, no need for two sets of propulsion machinery or for frequent surfacing; the reactor can be operated both at the surface and when the submarine is submerged.

Since the nuclear submarine may remain deeply submerged for weeks or even months, it cannot depend just on recycling to keep the air on board fit to breathe. So both fresh air and water are made on board. Fresh water is made by distilling seawater to remove the salt, while oxygen is made by electrolysis of fresh water, which generates oxygen and hydrogen.

The U.S. nuclear submarine *George Washington*.

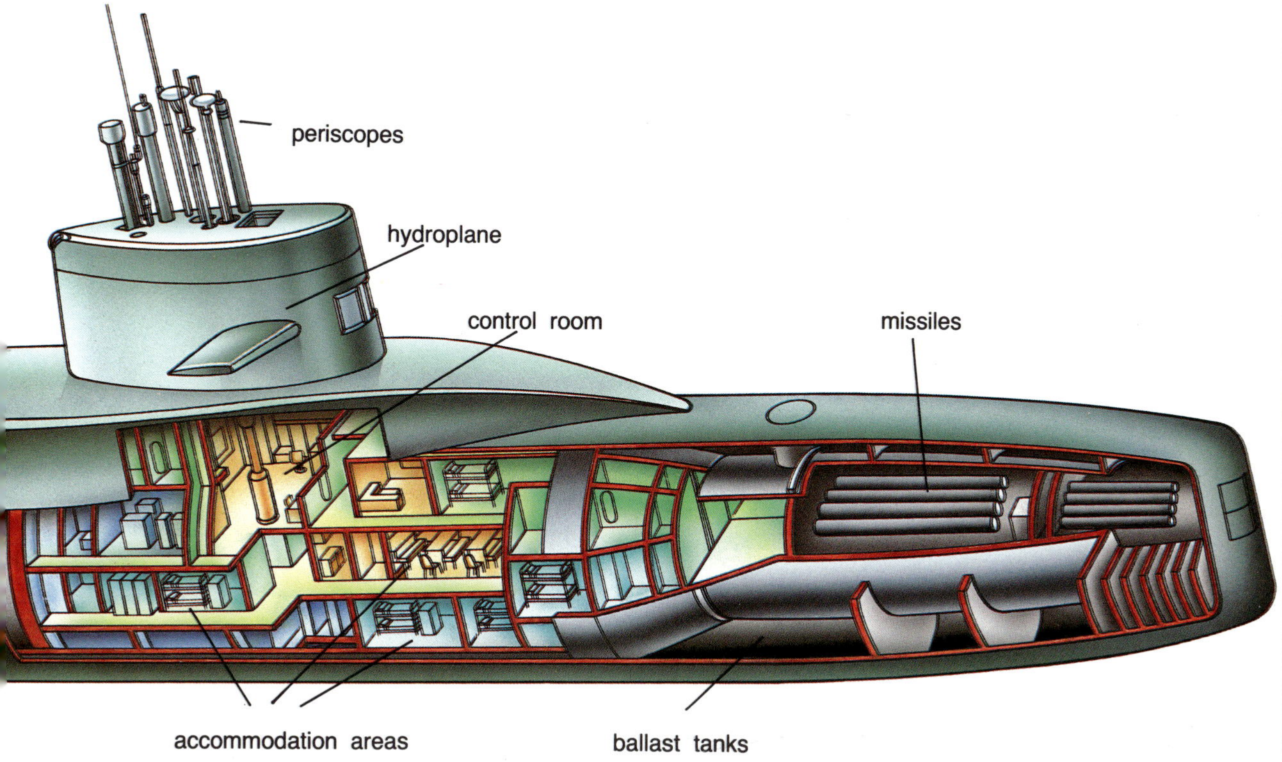

11 The bathyscaphe

Exploration of the deepest parts of the ocean requires a very special kind of vehicle that is highly pressure-resistant. The bottoms of the ocean canyons are well beyond the reach of conventional submarines because the pressure at such great depths would crush their cylindrical hulls despite the fact that they are constructed of thick steel.

Deep ocean trenches have been explored using a vehicle called a bathyscaphe. The bathyscaphe consists of a very strong steel sphere attached to the underside of a large main hull. The steel sphere is the cabin of the craft and it can accommodate just two crew. A spherical shape is used because it has been discovered that this gives the greatest strength for a given

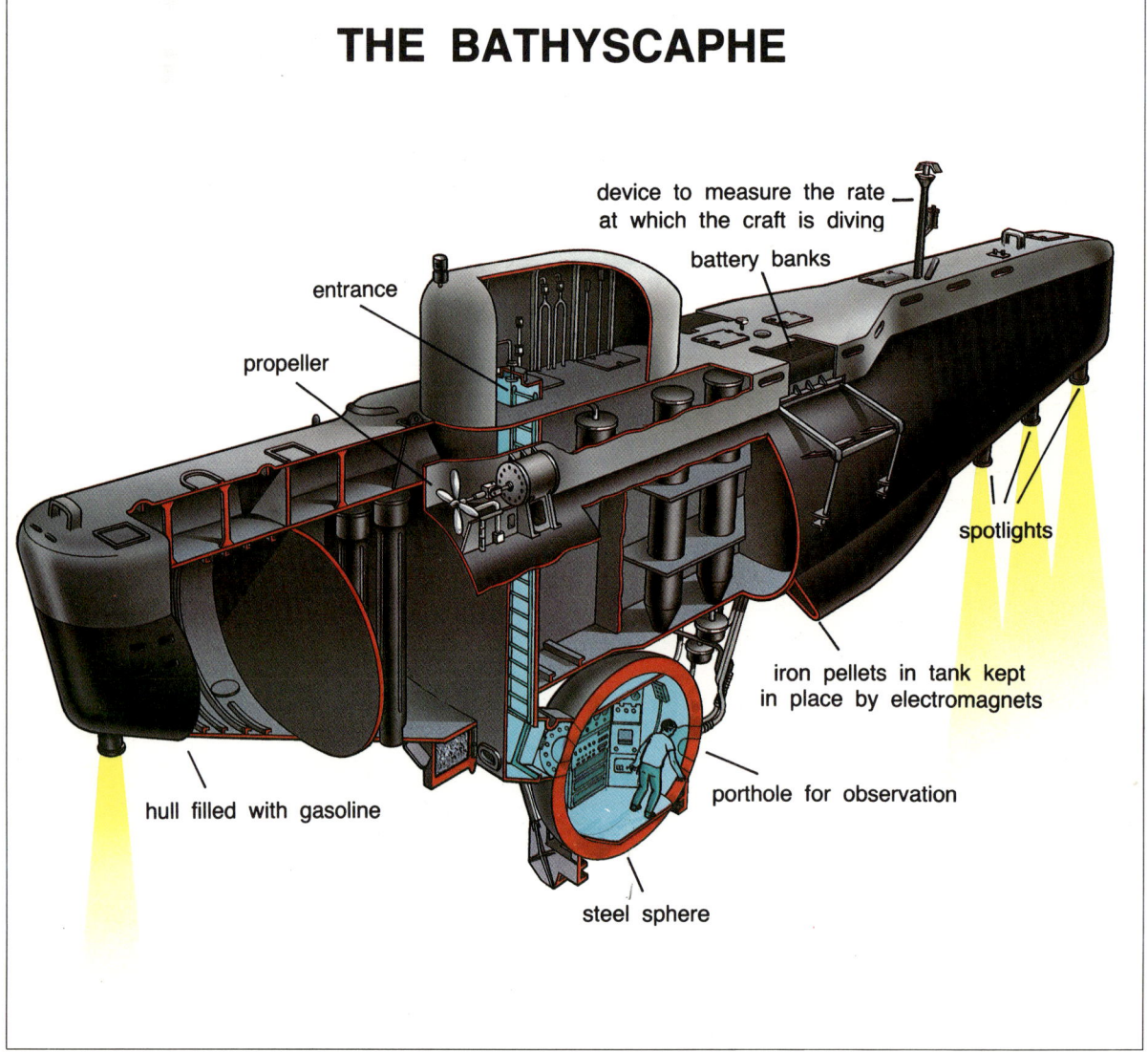

THE BATHYSCAPHE

- device to measure the rate at which the craft is diving
- battery banks
- entrance
- propeller
- spotlights
- iron pellets in tank kept in place by electromagnets
- porthole for observation
- steel sphere
- hull filled with gasoline

Professor August Picard prepares his bathyscaphe *Trieste* for a dive.

mass of steel. The large hull is used to provide the buoyancy needed to support the heavy steel sphere. This hull cannot be air filled because the great pressure would rupture or crush it, so instead it is filled with gasoline, which is less dense than water and so provides the craft with the necessary buoyancy.

As the craft dives toward the bottom of the ocean, fine adjustments are made to its buoyancy by releasing iron ballast pellets. To return to the surface after a deep dive, large amounts of ballast pellets are released, making the bathyscaphe float back up through the water. In very deep water, it is important that the bathyscaphe be able to return to the surface automatically should anything go wrong with its systems. For this reason, the ballast pellets are held in place by electromagnets, so that if there is a power failure on board the craft, all the pellets are automatically released and the bathyscaphe and its crew float safely to the surface.

The crew of the bathyscaphe are able to make observations through just one small porthole. Powerful lights are fitted to the craft to light up the seabed. The craft is also equipped with mechanical arms and probes for investigating the deep seafloor.

The deepest dive ever was carried out by the bathyscaphe *Trieste* back in January 1960. During this dive, the *Trieste* descended to a depth of 35,800 feet (10,912 m) in the Marianas Trench of the Pacific Ocean.

12 Undersea navigation

Navigation at the sea surface is achieved by a number of well-established methods. Close to land, ships can navigate by reference to landmarks on shore. Once out of sight of land, they make use of a wide range of radio navigation aids as well as radio signals, which are sent out by navigation satellites.

Beneath the sea surface none of these methods is possible unless the craft is close enough to the surface for landmarks to be visible through a periscope or for radio signals to be picked up by an antenna projecting above the sea surface. Submarines and all other undersea vessels, therefore, must use other means of navigating once they leave the surface.

One of the military advantages of nuclear submarines is that they can spend long periods of time at depths where they are almost impossible to detect. If they return near the surface to check their position, they are much more likely to be detected. What they need is a navigation system that can keep track of their position from the time they submerge to the time they resurface. The system that is used today is a modern version of one of the oldest navigation systems of all, "dead reckoning."

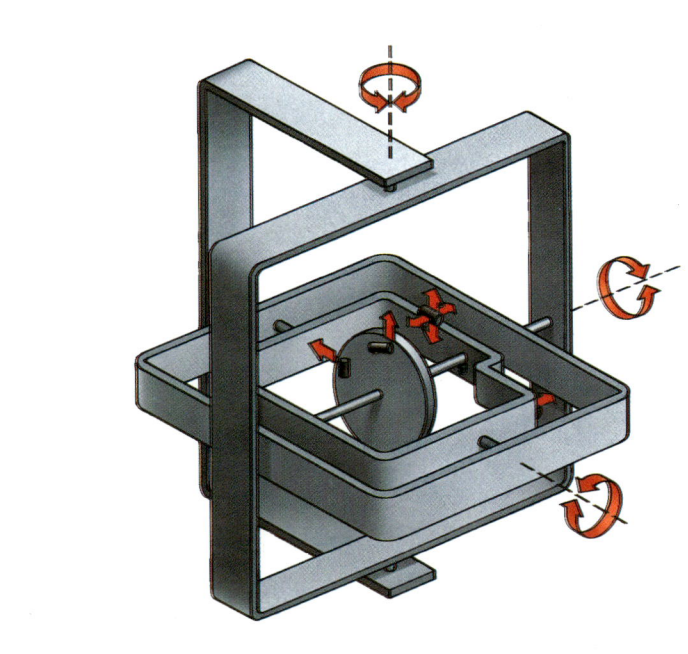

Gyroscopes keep their frames pointing north, east and straight up. When the vessel changes speed or course, the frames try to move. The force with which they try to move is measured. A computer analyzes the measurements to calculate the vessel's exact position.

Left The crew on board a submarine constantly monitor its position, which is calculated by the SINS (Ship's Inertial Navigation System).

The basic principle of "dead reckoning" is simple. If you know your starting point and you know how far you have traveled and in what direction, you can work out your new position. Modern gyro technology provides the means whereby a submerged submarine can constantly and very accurately measure changes of course and speed. This information can then be fed into a computer, which continuously calculates an accurate position for the craft. This method of navigation is known as a Ship's Inertial Navigation System, or SINS.

Other undersea vessels face different kinds of navigational problems. Submersibles and remotely operated vehicles carrying out underwater repair tasks often need to be able to determine their positions relative to the structure on which they are working. They achieve this using an acoustic positioning system. Sound pulses are sent to a series of transponders at known positions on the seafloor, and these transponders send a return sound pulse when they receive the pulse from the undersea vessel. A computer analyzes the times taken for the pulses to travel to and from each transponder in order to calculate the craft's correct position.

13 Fishing technology

By far the most important method of fishing is the use of some form of net operated from the side or the stern of a vessel. The technology of fishing nets has gradually improved over the years, as have the vessels used to operate them. Some of the nets are now so large and so efficient that they are capable of catching whole schools of fish in one go.

There have also been dramatic improvements in methods of locating fish. Until the application of electronics to fish-finding, locating schools of fish at sea was very much an art. Today, though,

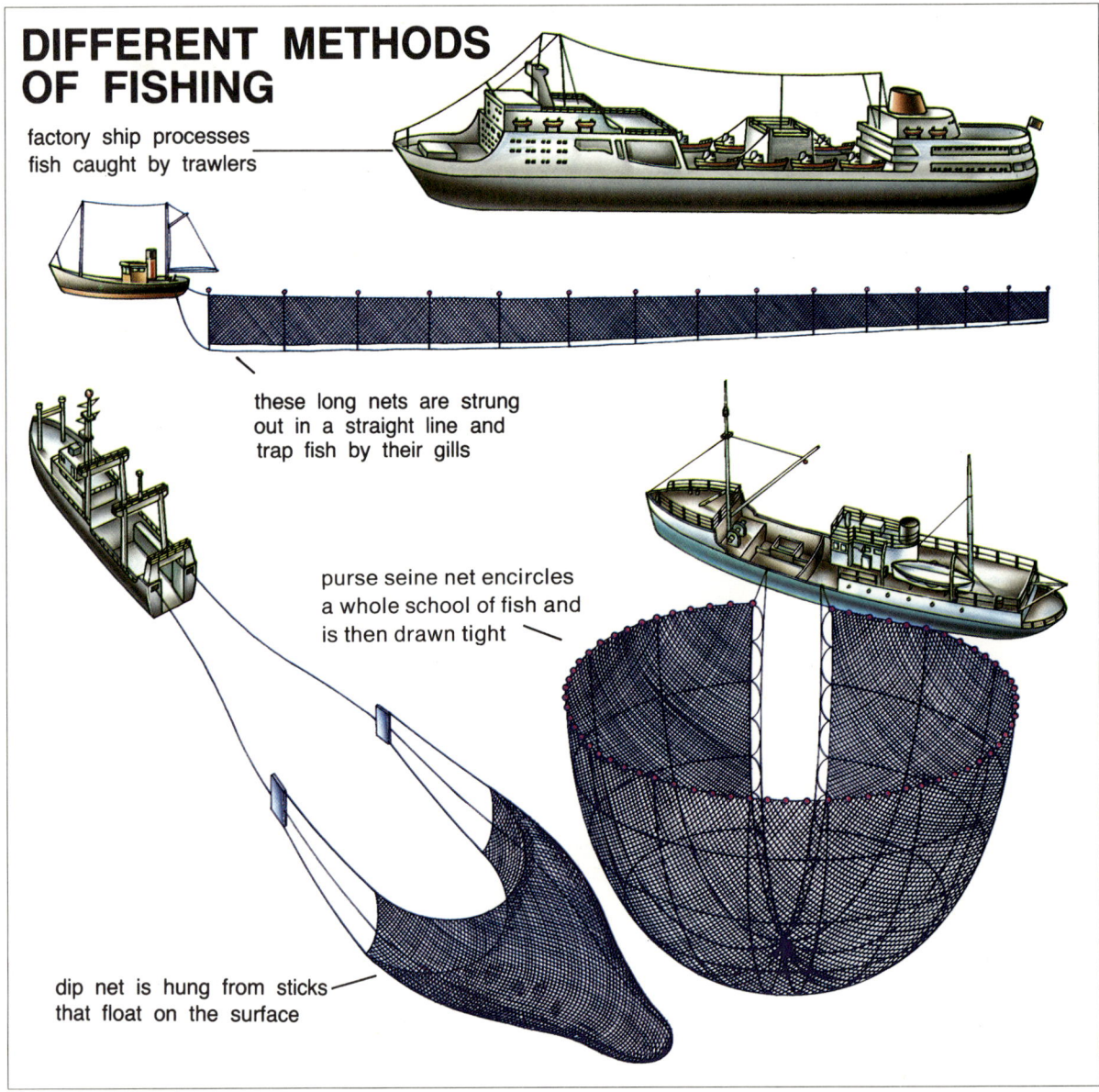

DIFFERENT METHODS OF FISHING

factory ship processes fish caught by trawlers

these long nets are strung out in a straight line and trap fish by their gills

purse seine net encircles a whole school of fish and is then drawn tight

dip net is hung from sticks that float on the surface

30

A fish farm in shallow coastal waters off Japan.

trawlers are equipped with a variety of electronic aids to make fish-finding a far more precise and scientific operation.

The fish-finding sonar is a development of the echo sounder. A conventional echo sounder will give an indication of the presence of a large school of fish, because the school will reflect the sound pulse and cause a weak echo to be detected at the surface. This appears on the echo sounder chart as a smudgy image above the line indicating the depth of the seabed. In advanced fish-finding sonars, the weaker echoes from schools of fish are electronically processed and displayed as a color image. Different colors give an indication of the density of the fish school. Some fish-finding sonars are also able to scan the waters ahead of the vessel.

The increasing efficiency with which wild fish are caught has resulted in serious pressure on our fish stocks. Fishing is now so efficient that uncontrolled exploitation can destroy a whole fishery through over-fishing.

One way of meeting the ever-increasing demand for food from the sea is to farm fish and shellfish, just as animals are farmed on land.

The origins of aquaculture can be traced back a long way. As long as 4,000 years ago, freshwater fish-farming was practiced in China. The earliest marine farmers were the Japanese, who began farming oysters and edible seaweeds centuries ago. Until recently, the development of farming methods for marine fish was limited by the difficulty of building cages strong enough to withstand the power of the waves and storms of the open sea. Using modern materials, however, it is now possible to build large holding cages that can be anchored in sheltered waters, such as bays and fjords. Fish farms of this type are used only for high-value fish such as sole, salmon and sea trout.

14 Offshore oil exploration

Once a prospective location for finding offshore oil or gas is identified from seismic exploration, the only way to test whether any oil or gas is actually present is to drill an exploration well. In the early days of offshore oil and gas exploration, wells were drilled only close to shore in water depths of no more than a few feet. These wells could be drilled using the same kinds of drilling rigs that were used on land.

It was not until the early 1960s that offshore oil and gas exploration began to move into the deeper waters of the continental shelf. The drilling of oil and gas wells away from the shoreline required the development of a whole new kind of technology.

The first type of offshore exploration drilling rig to be developed was the "jack-up" rig. This is a floating rig that is towed out to the drill site. Once there, legs are jacked down to the seabed and the entire drilling rig is lifted above the waves. Because there is a limit to the maximum length to which the legs can be extended before the structure becomes unstable, this type of rig can be used only in water depths of less than about 30 feet (100 m).

To drill exploration wells in deeper water, a different type of rig had to be designed. The solution was the semisubmersible rig, in which drilling equipment is positioned on a deck high above two very large shiplike hulls known as pontoons. Once in position at the drilling site, a semisubmersible is kept in place using huge anchors. There are usually two of these for each corner of the rig.

The semisubmersible is made into a stable drilling platform by partially filling the pontoons with seawater so that the whole structure settles to a level at which the pontoons are too deep to be affected by stormy waves at the surface. The submerged pontoons stabilize the drilling deck, allowing drilling to proceed.

Before starting to drill, it is necessary to put in place a massive valve that is designed to protect the drilling rig from any sudden release of high-pressure oil or gas that might occur during drilling. This special undersea valve is known as a "blowout preventer." It is located at the top of the well and it is designed to close automatically in the event of a sudden increase in pressure inside the well.

Drilling from a ship off the Brazilian coast. Ships are often used for exploration in deep waters.

During drilling, the drill bit is cooled and lubricated by specially prepared chemical "mud" that is pumped down the drill string used to rotate the bit. This mud passes back to the surface through the casing that surrounds the drill string. Geologists on board the rig examine the pieces of broken rock that are flushed out of the well. These can give important clues as to whether oil or gas is likely to be found at that particular site.

Right A blowout preventer valve on the deck of a drilling rig. The two men in the foreground give an indication of its size. **Below** A rig off the Australian coast, with one of its supply boats in the foreground.

15 Offshore oil production

Once a viable offshore oil or gas field has been discovered by exploratory drilling, the complex business of extracting the oil or gas and getting it to shore can begin. Most offshore production is carried out from structures fixed to the seafloor. These structures are used to drill production wells through which the oil and gas can flow to the surface. A typical platform may have up to thirty production wells. The problem with drilling straight down into the seabed is that only a comparatively small area can be exploited from one production platform. So special directional drilling techniques have been developed, allowing wells to be drilled through the seabed at an angle. This means wells can be made to enter the oil or gas reservoir some distance from the platform. In some cases, the platform may be connected by undersea pipeline to satellite wells, which enter the reservoir beyond the limits of directional drilling.

Besides being used to drill the wells, the production platform supports the whole range of complex machinery needed to handle the oil or gas. Operating and maintaining all this complex machinery requires many different skills; a large production platform may require a crew of several hundred people.

The majority of platforms in use today are supported on massive steel or concrete structures. These enormous structures are towed out

Above A crane barge lifts topside components into place on a production platform.
Right Many people are needed to operate a production platform.

to their final position, which can be in water depths of over 650 feet (198 m). Steel structures are pinned to the seafloor by long piles, which are driven into the seafloor by huge hammers.

Once the platform is in position, all the above-water components are attached to the portion of the structure that protrudes above the sea surface. These "topside" components are usually assembled into modules onshore. Each of the modules is lifted into place on the platform using huge floating cranes.

Aside from the difficulties of building and transporting these massive structures, there is also a limit to the depths at which they can work. So the latest generation of very deep-water platforms are supported not on rigid structures but on floating surface structures held in position by tensioned steel pipes fixed to frames attached to the seafloor by piles. These are known as tension leg platforms.

Once oil and gas are extracted from beneath the seafloor, some means must be found to transport them to the shore. In some cases this is done by using a tanker, which moors at a loading point at sea. More often the oil or gas is transported ashore through submarine pipelines. Pipelines are installed using vessels called lay barges. On board these vessels, the sections of pipe are welded one after another, covered with a protective coating, and lowered to the seabed over an arm known as a "stinger" at the stern of the vessel.

Oil and gas pipelines need regular inspection and cleaning. New kinds of technology have been developed to make possible the internal inspection and cleaning of hundreds of miles of pipeline. Pipelines are inspected and cleaned by robot devices called "pigs." These travel through the pipeline either cleaning the pipeline walls or, in the case of an inspection and testing pig, carrying out thousands of electronic measurements each second.

The U.S.-built Semac 1 pipe-laying barge.

16   Mining the seafloor

Modern society has an ever-growing need for supplies of sand and gravel for use in the construction industry. Much of this sand and gravel is now obtained from the shallow seafloor. Undersea sand and gravel are "mined" using dredgers. Several different types of dredgers can be used for this purpose. In very shallow water, the mining is usually done by a bucket dredger, a craft that scoops the material from the seafloor using a continuous chain of rotating buckets. The type of dredger most widely used for extracting aggregates is the suction hopper dredger. This vessel uses suction pumps to bring material up a tube from the seabed and deposit it in a large hopper on board.

Although sands and gravels are the most commonly mined undersea materials, many other valuable mineral resources are also found on the seafloor. In some locations, coastal sands are rich in minerals such as tin and, at some sites (off the South African coast, for example), diamonds. In offshore diamond mining, dredged seabed material is brought up and sorted on board a custom-designed dredger.

Much effort has gone into exploring the mineral riches of the deep ocean beyond the coastal waters. Observation from undersea craft has shown that large areas of the deep ocean floor are covered with a carpet of potato-shaped nodules that are rich in minerals such as manganese. At other locations, seamounts have been found to have valuable mineral deposits on their sides.

Commercial mining of these deposits has yet

These rows of buckets on a dredger are used to scoop up seabed material.

Manganese nodules covering the deep seabed.

to take place, due to the problems of operating mining machinery at great depths and pressures, and the difficulties of lifting huge quantities of material up from the seafloor to the surface. Considerable work has, however, been done to investigate means of overcoming these obstacles, and several prototype mining machines have been developed.

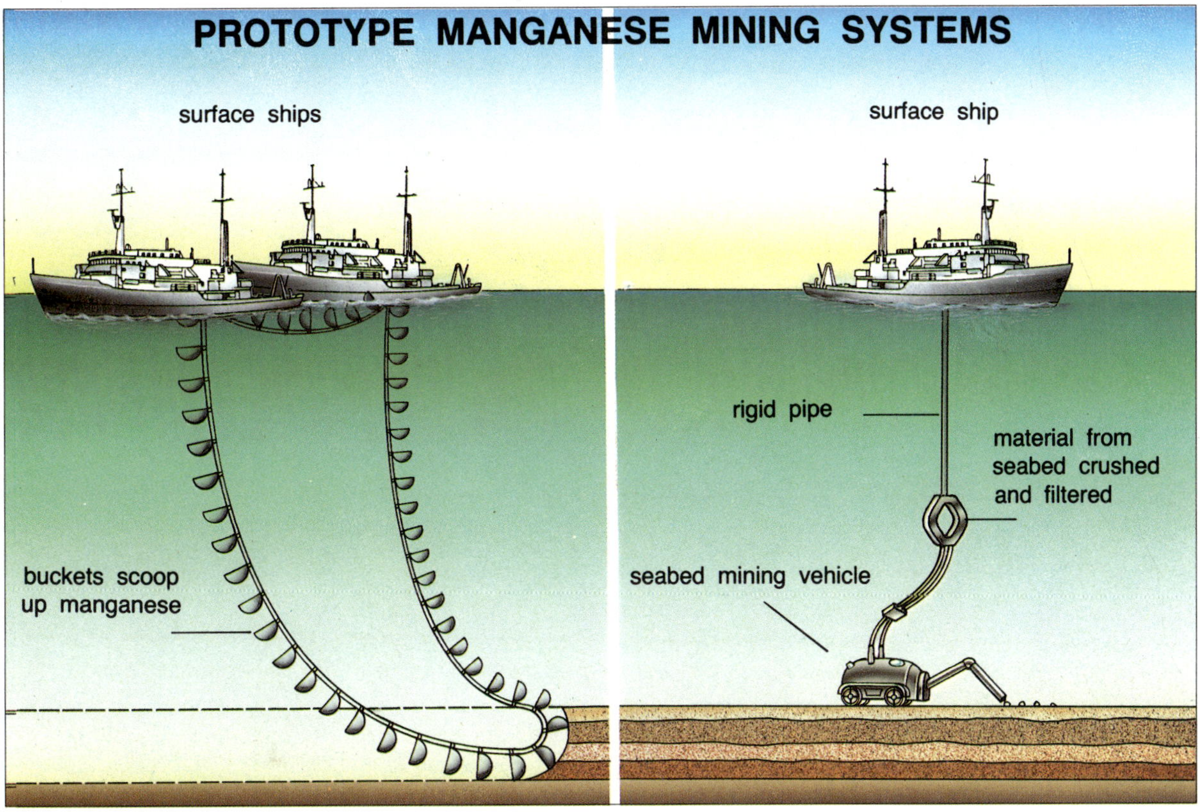

PROTOTYPE MANGANESE MINING SYSTEMS

surface ships

buckets scoop up manganese

surface ship

rigid pipe

material from seabed crushed and filtered

seabed mining vehicle

17 Energy from the sea

Above La Rance tidal barrage in Brittany, France. The sluice gates in the foreground in the picture on the right let the tide flow in through the barrage.

The concept of generating power by harnessing the energy of tides has been with us for a long time. For many centuries, the energy in tides was used on a small scale in tide mills for grinding grain or cutting wood. The technology that has made it possible to use this energy at sites away from the shore is, however, far more recent, depending as it does on the transformation of tidal energy into electrical energy.

There are a number of sites around the world where the rise and fall of the tide is sufficient to make tidal power-generation a practical possibility (the Bay of Fundy on the eastern coast of Canada, for example, and the Severn Estuary in Britain).

The principles of a tidal power station are really quite simple. A barrage is built between two locations on the coast, separating a large volume of water from the open sea. Sluice gates in the barrage are opened for the incoming rising tide, allowing the basin created by the barrage to fill with water. At high tide, the sluice gates are closed. When the water level outside the barrage has fallen sufficiently, water is allowed to flow out to the sea, passing through turbines and so generating electricity.

Waves generated by the wind blowing over the sea surface carry considerable energy, as is often apparent from the damage they can cause along the coastline. Very small-scale wave power generation has been used for some time to provide power to recharge the batteries of offshore navigation buoys, but there are still many problems to be overcome before wave power devices can be operated on a large scale.

A novel source of energy from the sea is to tap the energy of ocean thermal gradients. In deep tropical waters, there is a constant large temperature difference between the surface waters, which are heated by the intense tropical sunlight, and the cold deep water. By using the surface waters to heat a fluid with a low boiling point, like ammonia, vapor can be generated to drive a turbine. Cold, deep water can then be used to condense the vapor and the cycle can be repeated indefinitely. As with wave power devices, such power generation has yet to be demonstrated on a large scale.

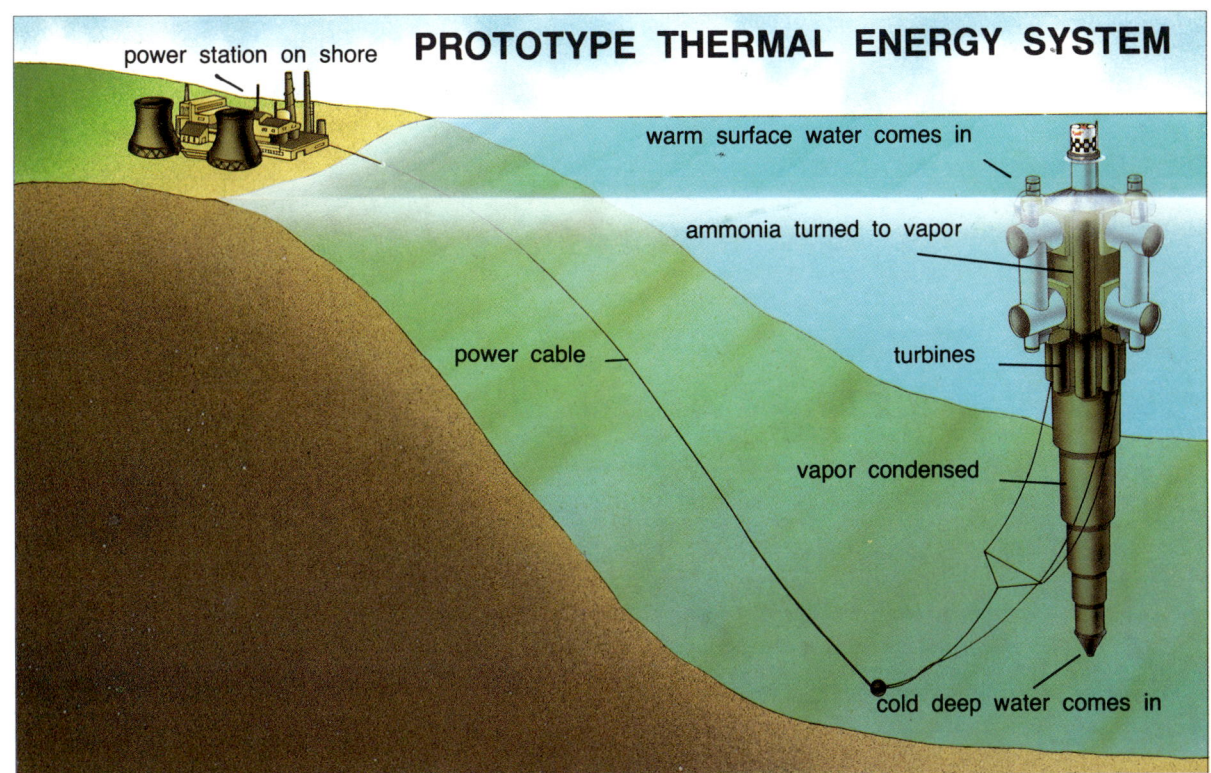

18 Protecting the environment

Our exploitation of the oceans and seas brings many benefits but it is not without its problems. The growing demand for marine resources and the use of the oceans and seas for the disposal of waste is placing the marine environment under ever greater pressure.

To safeguard the environment, our use of the oceans and seas must be carefully regulated and managed. Technology developed to exploit the wealth of oceans must also be carefully designed to minimize the risk of harming the environment in which it operates. Despite the national and international regulations that exist to protect the environment, damaging pollutants are still released into the sea, either deliberately (when oil tankers illegally wash out their storage tanks at sea, for example) or as the result of accidents.

One of the most significant risks to the marine environment is oil pollution. There is the risk of oil spills from offshore oil drilling and production, and potentially enormous damage can be done to the environment as a result of accidents involving large oil tankers. The threat of oil

An oil skimmer lowered over the side of a ship sucks up polluted water.

pollution has led to the development of technology to assist in the monitoring and control of accidental spillages at sea.

When an oil spill occurs, it is necessary to be able to predict and monitor its speed. Predicting the spread of an oil slick relies on a good knowledge of weather conditions and currents. Details about the latter can be discovered using strategically placed undersea current meters. Weather and current information is used in computer programs that forecast the path that a floating oil slick will follow and assess the risk of contamination of the shoreline. The actual progress of a slick is often monitored from the air using aircraft fitted with special cameras that help to show up the oil more clearly.

Many devices have been designed to help with cleaning up and containing floating oil slicks. They are often contained using long floating booms that are laid around the oil slick to prevent it from spreading. The oil is then removed from the surface using devices a little like giant vacuum cleaners in appearance.

Unfortunately, the devices designed to clean up oil spills do not work very well in rough seas, and in some cases the only way to control a floating oil slick is to spray it with detergents, which help to break it down. Detergents have the disadvantage, though, that they too can be harmful to marine life.

In addition to the risks of oil pollution, there are many other threats to the marine environment, including the release of toxic chemicals and the problems of over-exploitation of living resources. These threats to the environment must be constantly monitored and controlled.

Booms contain an oil slick off the western coast of the United States.

19 A future undersea?

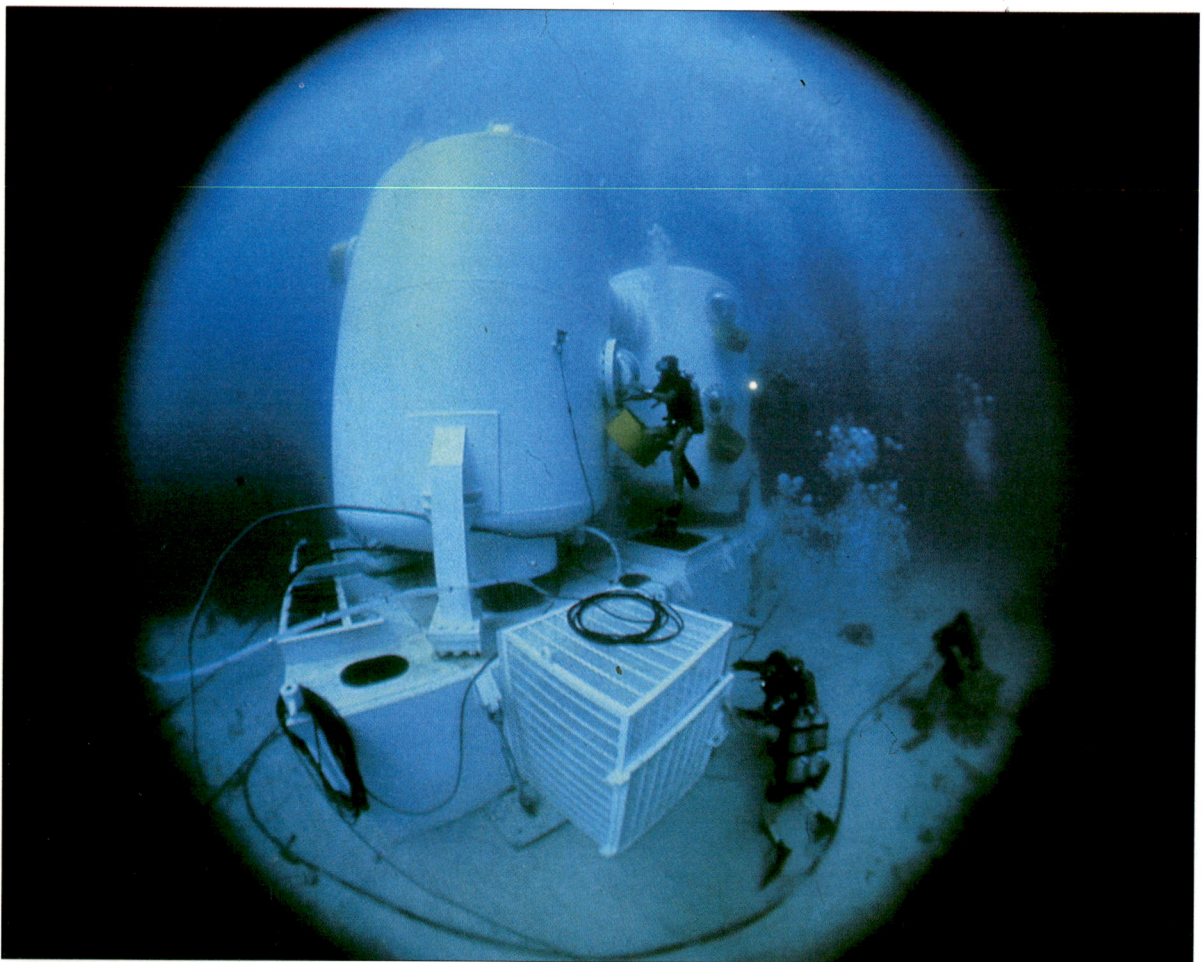

Divers working around the Tektite experimental undersea habitat off the U.S. coast.

As more and more of the limited resources available on the land are used up, attention will increasingly turn to marine resources and the development of the technology required to exploit them. Machines will have to be designed to work in very deep waters to allow the mining and recovery of deep seabed minerals such as manganese. In the oil and gas industries, the search for new fields is taking us to ever greater depths, depths that are simply too great to be exploited using the conventional production platform operated from the surface. Instead, all of the production equipment will have to be located on the seafloor. Much of the technology currently being developed to allow oil production in these depths will form a basis for developments required to exploit the resources of the very deep ocean.

As our attention turns to the exploration and exploitation of ever deeper waters in which enabling humans to work becomes highly difficult, robot machines will be of increasing importance. Because of the great depths at which these machines will be required to work, it will not be possible to tether them to the surface, and communication and control links will not be viable. Instead, they will have to be completely self-controlled and programmed to perform complex undersea tasks before returning themselves to the surface. Computer technology will therefore assume an even greater role in undersea exploration and production.

In the future, people will also need to live and work on the ocean floor for long periods of time, both to observe and monitor the undersea world and to supervise commercial operations such as mining. This will involve the building of sophisticated undersea habitats, with areas set aside for accommodation and for the housing of production or scientific equipment. Some experimental undersea habitats have been used in shallow continental-shelf waters, and it seems certain that humans will some day live at great depths under the oceans.

The future of undersea technology poses many exciting challenges if the problems of exploring and exploiting the inner space of this water-covered planet are to be overcome.

Left Undersea habitats allow divers to conduct marine experiments without constantly having to return to the surface.

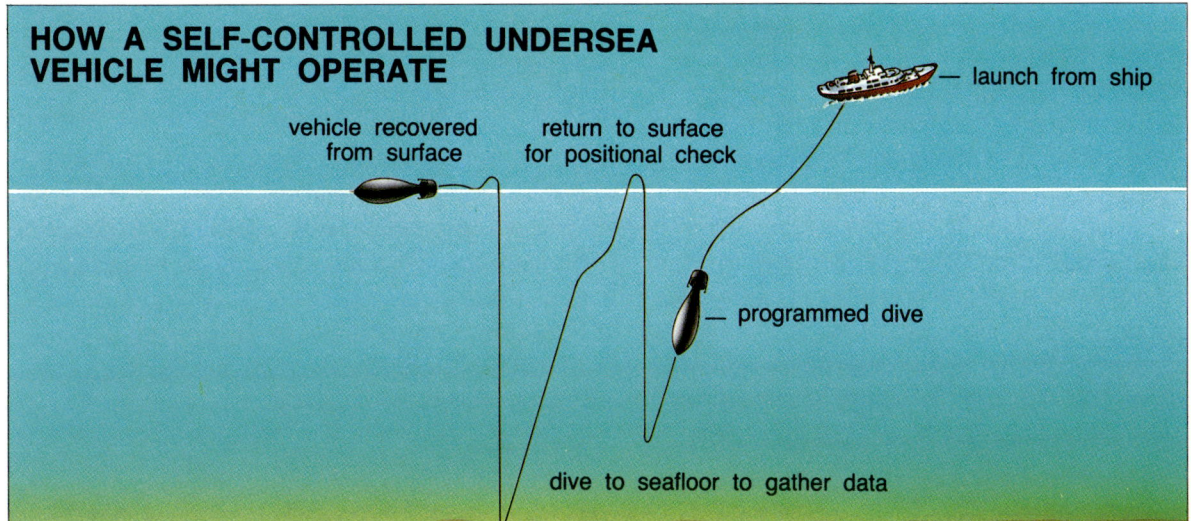

Glossary

Abyssal Of the deeper parts of the oceans beyond the continental shelf.
Aggregate A mixture of stones, gravel, sand and other hard materials, mixed with cement to make concrete.
Airgun A device that uses compressed air to generate underwater shock waves.
Alloy A mixture of two or more metals, produced to improve their overall strength or quality.
Aquaculture The controlled growing of animals and plants in water.
Ballast Tank A water tank that can be filled or emptied for diving and surfacing.
Barrage An artificial barrier across a river or estuary.
Boom A long, partly submerged tube used in containing oil slicks.
Continental Shelf The underwater plain bordering the continents.
Corrosive A corrosive substance is one that chemically attacks other materials, in the way that seawater attacks steel, causing rust.
Decompression The gradual reduction of pressure surrounding a diver who is coming to the surface, allowing time for the gas that has built up in his bloodstream to be released without harm.
Distilling The heating of a liquid until it becomes a gas, and the cooling of the gas so that it becomes a liquid again. This process separates the liquid from materials dissolved in it.
Diving Bell A pressurized chamber in which a diver is lowered to the working depth.
Echo Sounder An apparatus for measuring the depth of seas. Sound waves are transmitted through the water, and the time it takes for an echo to be sent back from the seabed is used to calculate the water's depth.

Electrolysis The process of breaking down a liquid into its chemical parts by passing an electric current through it. Electrolysis of water separates the water into oxygen and hydrogen gas.
Electromagnet A magnet whose force field is created by an electric current. If the current fails, the magnet loses its force.
Elements Substances that cannot be broken down into simpler substances.
Gantry A frame used for lifting and lowering craft into the sea.
Geological Concerning the study of the Earth's crust and its rocks.
Gyro A rotating wheel whose axis is free to turn but which maintains a fixed direction unless an external force acts upon it.
Hard Hat An early diving helmet that had to be supplied with compressed air from a surface pump.
Hydraulic Powered by the movement of a fluid.
Hydrophones Underwater microphones.
Minerals Inorganic substances that occur naturally in the Earth. Combinations of minerals form rocks.
Module A self-contained building unit that can be attached to structures like oil platforms.
Nitrogen Narcosis A feeling like drunkenness caused by breathing nitrogen gas at high pressure.
Oceanography Scientific study of the oceans.
Pneumatic Powered by a compressed gas (usually air).
Pressure Chamber A chamber in which the pressure inside can be kept at a different level from the pressure outside.
Seamounts Individual submarine mountains.
Sediment Solid matter that settles at the bottom of a liquid.

Seismic Exploration Investigating the nature of sediments and rocks beneath the sea-floor by studying the way in which sound passes through them and is reflected by them.

Transponder An electronic device that transmits a signal in reply to a coded signal.

Turbine A steam-, air- or water-driven wheel used to generate electricity or to drive propellers.

Umbilical A pipe from the surface supplying air, and sometimes warm water and communication links, to divers and some undersea craft.

Further reading

The Dying Sea by Michael Bright (Watts, 1988)
Life in the Sea by Philip Steele (Watts, 1986)
The Oceans by Martyn Bramwell (Watts, 1987)
The Oceans by David Lambert (Bookwright, 1987)
Oceanography by Martyn Bramwell (Watts, 1989)
Research Satellites by D. J. Herda (Watts, 1987)
Technology: Science at Work by Robin McKie (Watts, 1984)
Undersea Archaeology by Christopher Lampton (Watts, 1988)
Water Ecology by Jennifer Cochrane (Bookwright, 1987)
The World's Oceans by Cass R. Sandak (Watts, 1987)

Picture Acknowledgments

The publishers would like to thank the following for allowing their photographs to be used in this book: Oxford Scientific Films 6, 38 (bottom), 41; Planet Earth Pictures *front cover*, 11, 16, 19, 22, 23, 31, 32, 37, 42, 43; Ralph Rayner 40; Ann Ronan Picture Library 10 (left); Royal Navy Flag Office 28; Science Photo Library 9, 10 (right); Shell Photographic Library 5, 12, 13, 14, 17, 33, 34, 35, 37; Topham 25, 27, 36, 38 (top); ZEFA 20. All artwork is by the Ron Hayward Group.

Index

abyssal ocean 5, 44
accidents 40
acoustic positioning 29
aggregates 36, 44
aircraft 41
airguns 8, 44
air recycling 13, 24, 25
Alvin 23
ammonia 39
aquaculture 31, 44
Aristotle 10
Australia 33

ballasts 18, 27, 44
barrages 39, 44
bathyscaphes and bathyspheres 18, 26–7
battery power 23, 24
bends, the 11
blowout preventers 32, 33
booms 41, 44
Brazil 32
breathing underwater 5, 10, 11, 12, 13, 14, 22, 24, 25
Britain 4, 39
buoyancy 18–19, 27

cameras 6, 7, 21, 23, 41
Canada 39
canyons 26
Challenger, HMS 4, 6
charting and mapping 6, 7
Chile 4
China 31
claws 23
communications 12, 13, 43
compressed air 8, 10, 17, 19
computers 9, 11, 29, 41, 43
continental shelf 4, 20, 32, 43, 44
continental slope 4

corrosion 5, 6, 44
Cousteau, Jacques-Yves 10
cranes 34, 35

dead reckoning 28
decompression 11, 13, 14, 23
decompression chambers 14, 23
demand valves 10
depth measurement 6, 7
detergents 41
diamonds 36
diesel engines 24
distillation 25, 44
diving 10–16, 20, 22
diving bells 10, 13, 14, 44
diving support vessels 13
dredgers 36
drilling 5, 9, 32, 33, 34, 40
dynamic positioning 9

echo sounders 6, 7, 31, 44
electricity 16, 39
electrocution 16, 17
electrolysis 25, 44
electromagnets 27, 44
electronics 6, 7, 8, 12, 30, 31, 35
energy 5, 38–9
exploration 4, 6–7, 8–9, 23, 26, 32–3, 34, 42
exploration rigs 32–3
explosives 8

fishing 5, 30-31
fish-finding sonar 31
France 24, 38
Fundy, Bay of 39

gantries 23, 44

garages 21
gasoline 27
George Washington 25
GLORIA 7
grabs 7, 23
gravel 36
gyros 29, 44

habitats 42, 43
hard hats 10, 44
helium 12
hulls 26, 32
hydraulics 17, 23, 44
hydrogen 25
hydrophones 8, 9, 44
hydroplanes 19

Iceland 5

jack-up rigs 32
Japan 31
Jarrett, Jim 14
Jason Junior 23
JIM suits 14, 15
joysticks 20

lay barges 35
light 6, 7, 27

manganese 5, 36, 37, 42, 44
manipulator arms 23, 27
Marianas Trench 27
metals 6, 17, 26
mid-ocean ridges 4, 5
minerals 5, 36, 37, 42, 44
mining 36–7, 42, 43
modules 35, 44
mother ships 22, 23
motors 9, 17, 19, 23, 24
"mud" 33

Narval 24
Nautilus 24
navigation 28–29
navigation buoys 39
Nigeria 12
nitrogen narcosis 11, 12, 44
North Sea 22
Norway 5
nuclear power 19, 24, 25

oceanography 4, 6, 44
oil and gas 5, 32–5, 40, 41, 42
oil slicks 41
oil skimmers 40
one-atmosphere suits 14
over-exploitation 31, 40
oxygen 11, 12, 25
oxygen poisoning 11, 12

Pacific Ocean 27
periscopes 24, 28
Picard, August 27
pigs 35
piles 35
pipelines 34, 35
pneumatic power 17, 44
pollution 40, 41
pontoons 32
pressure 5, 6, 7, 10, 11, 12, 14, 17, 21, 22, 26, 27, 32, 37
pressure chambers 14, 22, 44
probes 27
production platforms 16, 17 18, 34–5, 40, 42

propellers 9, 19, 21, 24, 25
prototypes 37, 39, 43
pumps 10, 17, 36

radio signals 28
Rance, La 38
remotely operated vehicles 18, 19, 20–21, 23, 29
resources 4–5, 30–37, 40, 42
rock layers 8, 9
rotors 17
rudders 19

sand 36
satellites 28
saturation diving 14
scrubbers 24
SCUBA equipment 10
seamounts 36, 44
sediment 17, 44
seismic surveying 8, 9, 32, 44
semisubmersible rigs 32
Severn Estuary 39
Siberia 4
side-scan sonar 7
SINS 29
sluice gates 38, 39
snorkel tubes 24
sonar beacons 9
sonar imaging 7
sound 6, 7, 8, 9, 17, 29, 31
sounding leads 6, 7
South Africa 36
stingers 35

submarines 18, 19, 23, 24–5, 26, 28
submersibles 18, 19, 22–3, 29

tankers 35, 40
Tektite 42, 43
television 20
tension leg platforms 35
thermal gradients 39
thermal lances 16
thrusters 9, 21
tides 5, 38, 39
tin 36
Titanic 23
tools 16, 17, 21, 23
topsides 34, 35
towfish 7
transponders 9, 29, 44
trawlers 30
Trieste 27
turbines 25, 39, 44

umbilicals 12, 13, 20, 23, 44
United States 9, 24, 25, 35, 41, 42

waste disposal 40
waves 31, 39
welding 17
working underwater 13, 14, 16–17, 22, 23